NOT ME

ELISE GRAVEL

North Winds Press
An Imprint of Scholastic Canada Ltd.

For Luca.

This is a work of fiction.
Any resemblance to actual
events or persons is
entirely coincidental.

Library and Archives Canada Cataloguing in Publication

Title: Not me / Elise Gravel.

Other titles: Pas moi! English

Names: Gravel, Elise, author, illustrator.

Description: Translation of: Pas moi! | Published simultaneously in softcover by Scholastic Canada Ltd.

Identifiers: Canadiana 20200205749 | ISBN 9781443181747 (hardcover)

Classification: LCC PS8563.R3876 P3714 2020 | DDC jC843/.6—dc23

www.scholastic.ca

6 5 4 3 2 1   Printed in Canada 114   20 21 22 23 24 25

NOT ME

ELISE GRAVEL

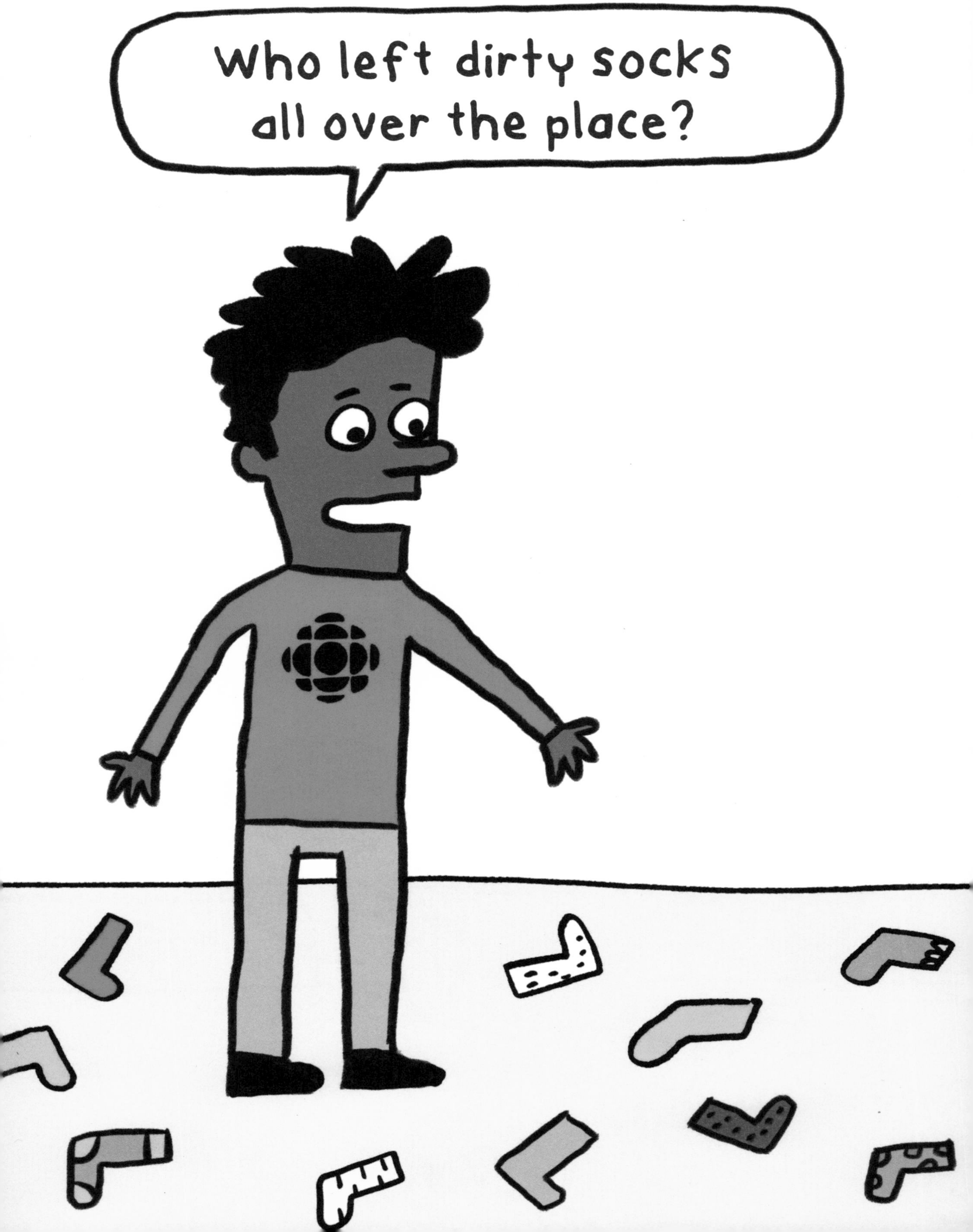
Who left dirty socks all over the place?

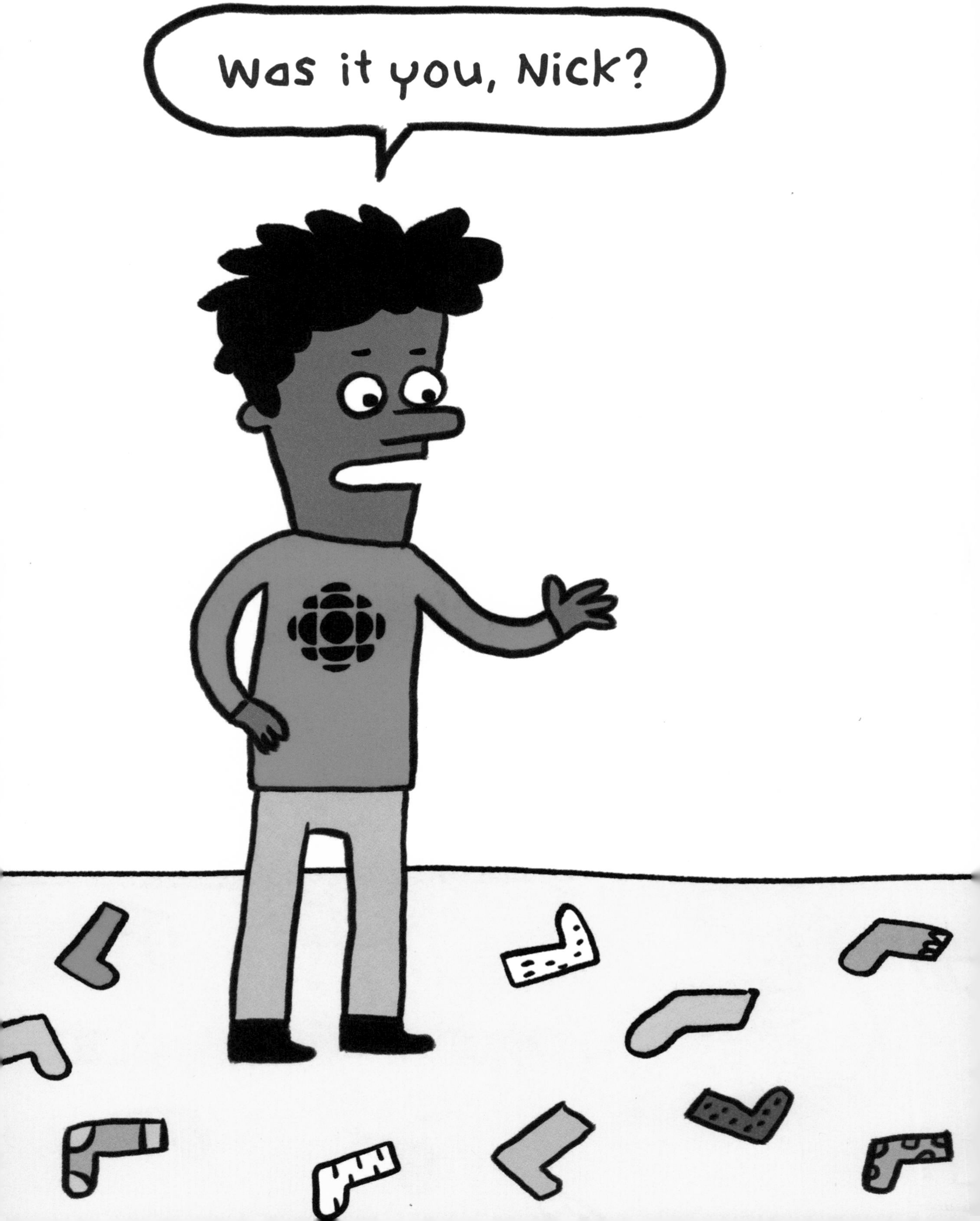
Was it you, Nick?

Somebody is not telling the truth. And unless someone does,

BOTH OF YOU

will get a time out.

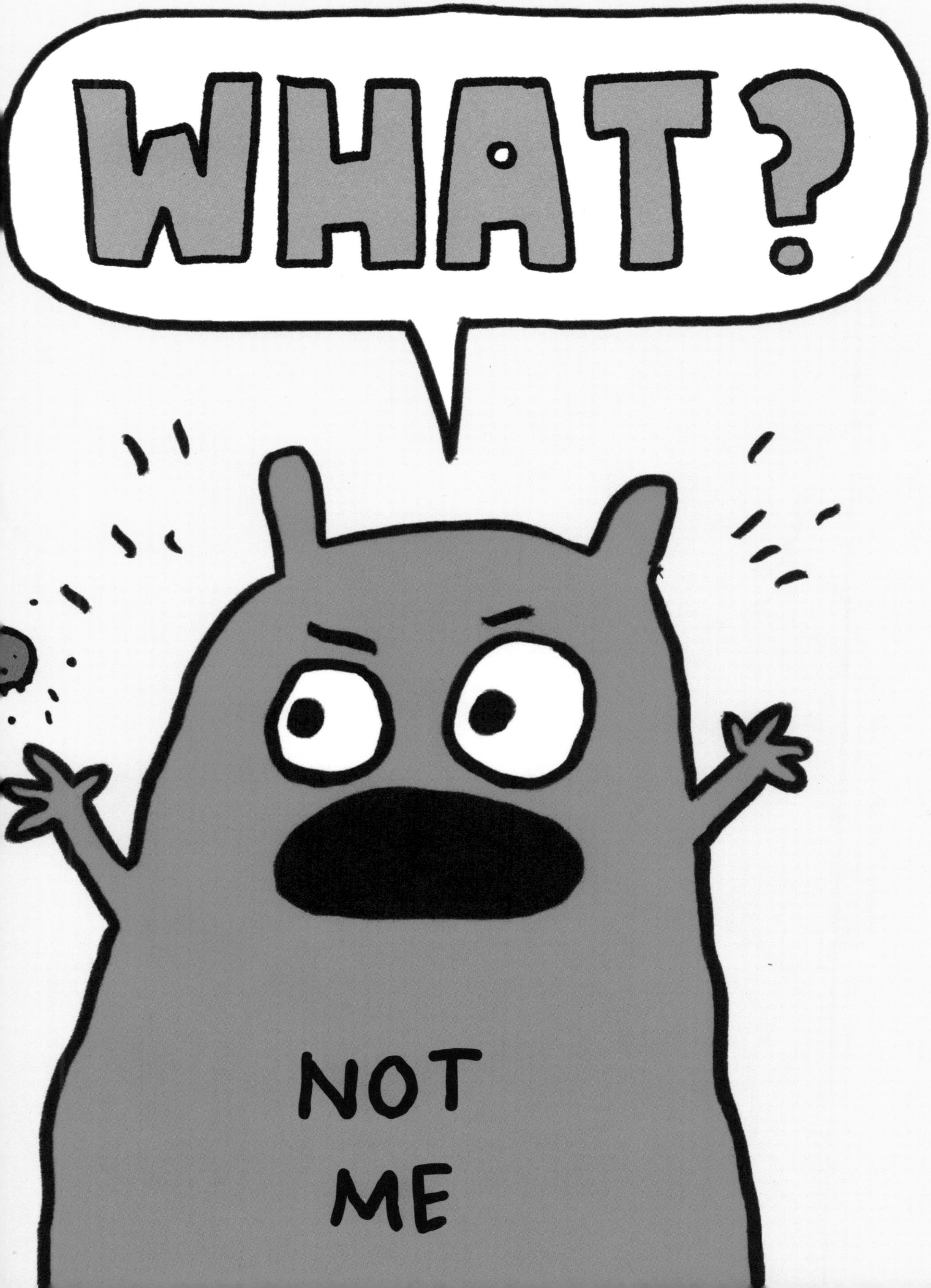
WHAT?
NOT ME

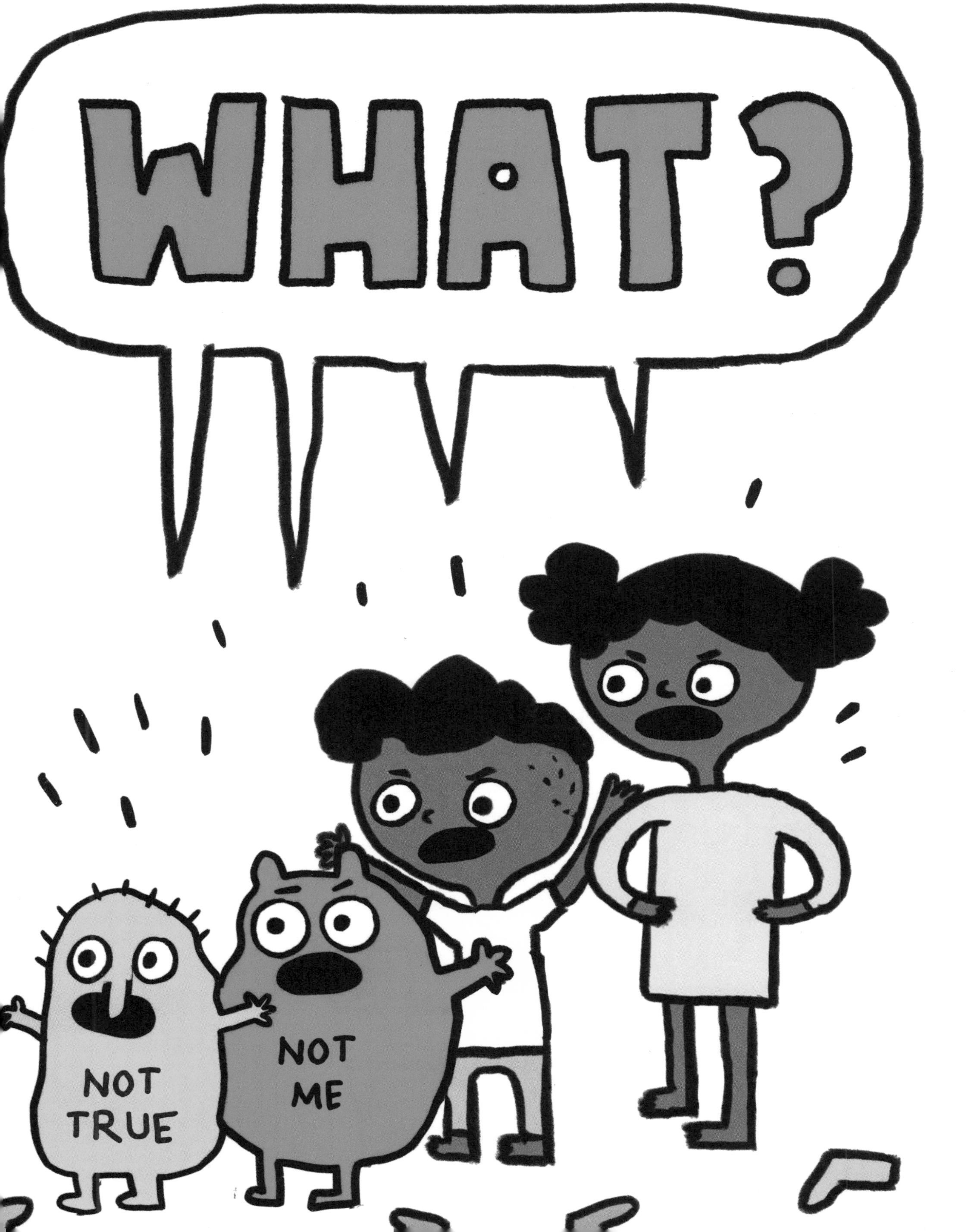
WHAT?
NOT TRUE
NOT ME